Centipede's 100 Shoes

1 2 3 4 5 6 7 8 9 10 11 12 13 14 15 16 17 18 19 20 21 22 23 24 25 26 27 28 29 30 31 32 33 34 35 36 37 38 39 40 41 42 43 44 45 46 47 48 49 50 51 52 53 54 55 56 57 58 59 60 61 62 63 64 65 66 67 68 69 70 71 72 73 74 75 76 77 78 79 80 81 82 83 84 85 86 87 88 89 90 91 92 93 94 95 96 97 98 99 100

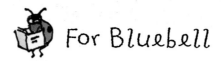 For Bluebell

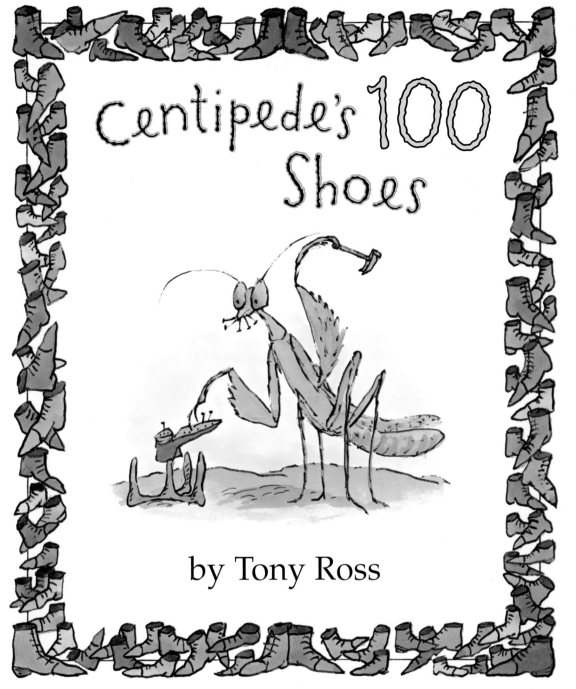

Centipede's 100 Shoes

by Tony Ross

Andersen Press
London

10   9

British Library Cataloguing in Publication Data available.

ISBN 978 184270 284 0

This book has been printed on acid-free paper

"Ow!"
The little centipede was not looking where he was going,
and he hurt his toe.

But which one? "Mum will know!"
Not this one, or this one, or this one, or this one,
or this one, or this one, or this one . . .

"Come here and I'll kiss it better," said Mum.

At last, Mum found the hurt toe, and kissed it better.
"Tomorrow, you must get some shoes," she said.

Early next morning, his mum took the little centipede
to the shoe shop.

"One hundred shoes, please!" said the little centipede.
"Fifty left ones, and fifty right ones."

"Why do you want one hundred?" said the shoe seller.
"Because I'm a centipede, which means a hundred legs,"
said the little centipede.

"Do you want lace-ups, or buckles?" asked the shoe seller. "Lace-ups, please," said the little centipede. "Lace-ups are more grown up."

So the little centipede tried on shoes until he found ones
that he liked, and the shoe salesman wrapped them up.

The next day, the little centipede put on his shoes.
It took a long time. Then he had to tie up all the laces,
and when at last he had finished . . .

. . . he had fifty-eight shoes left over.

"That's because most centipedes have only forty-two legs," said his grandad.

When the last shoe was laced up, it was bedtime and time to start taking the shoes off again.

Next morning, the little centipede put on his shoes again. This time he was quicker, and he was better at tying the laces.

So after lunch, he went for a walk.
"Oh, Mum!" he cried. "My new shoes hurt!"

"That's because you have no socks on," said his mother.
And the little centipede started to take off his shoes again . . .

. . . and his aunties all began to knit socks.

Next morning, the little centipede put on all his socks.
He had his lunch, then started to put on his shoes.

Just before supper, he went for a walk.
"All my feet feel fine now, Mum," he said.
"Time for bed," said his mother.

So the little centipede took off his shoes and tumbled into bed.
"You can't go to sleep in your socks!" said his mother.
So he took off his socks as well.

Next morning, the little centipede looked at all the shoes and socks.

"Oh, I don't think I'll bother!" he sighed.

So he put his one hundred shoes, and his forty-two socks into his little barrow . . .

. . . and sold them all to creepy-crawlies with fewer legs. He sold shoes to five spiders, four beetles, two woodlice, and a grasshopper . . .

. . . with socks for the five spiders,

and with enough shoes and socks left

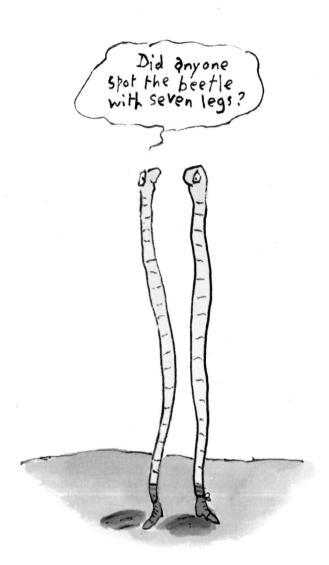

. . . for two worms.